RABBIT TALES

SNOW GOOSE SPECIAL

A Unicorn Book • E. P. Dutton • New York

RABBIT TALES

by John E. McCormack • pictures by Jenni Oliver

Library of Congress Cataloging in Publication Data

McCormack, John E.   Rabbit tales.
(A Unicorn book)
SUMMARY: Six rabbits traveling by train to Elderberry for the
Easter holiday pass the time by telling tales of rabbits.
[1. Rabbits—Fiction.   2. Short stories]
I. Oliver, Jenni.   II. Title.
PZ7.M13675Rab   1980   [E]   79-20089   ISBN 0-525-38005-1

Published in the United States by E. P. Dutton, a Division
of Elsevier-Dutton Publishing Company, Inc., New York

Published simultaneously in Canada by Clarke,
Irwin & Company Limited, Toronto and Vancouver

Editor: Emilie McLeod   Designer: Riki Levinson

Printed in the U.S.A.   First Edition
10 9 8 7 6 5 4 3 2 1

to Marie
and our five children,
Kathi, Jack, Peggi, Ellen, and Claire

CONTENTS

Once there were six rabbits
traveling by train
to Elderberry
for the Easter holidays.
"We will be traveling all night,"
  said the conductor.
"So make yourselves comfortable."

"Well then,"
  said one of the six rabbits,
"let us each tell a tale
  to pass away the time.
  Whoever tells the best tale
  will win a large basket full of Easter eggs."

The other rabbits agreed,
and so the tales began....

The First Rabbit removed her little flowered bonnet
and started her tale.

THREE HARES AND THEIR BEAUTIFUL HATS

Down at the end of Blackberry Lane,
in a house full of beautiful hats,
there lived three hares.
The three hares loved hats so much
that they had no time at all
for friends or fun or even for work.
Every day they would sit before their mirror
primping and posing until, finally,
the old mirror would mutter grumpily,
"I am tired!" and he would fall asleep.

One Easter morning
none of the three hares could choose the right hat
to wear in the Easter Parade.
So they turned to their mirror and said,
"Mirror, Mirror, on the wall,
which three bonnets are most beautiful of all?"
But the old mirror was sound asleep.

With that,
the three hares stacked on all their flowered hats
and marched proudly down the street.

"How fine we look," they said to one another
as they marched through the park
and stopped by the pond to admire themselves.
TIPPLE! TIPPLE! TOPPLE! FLIP!
Down fell all the hats into the pond.
The hares smiled foolish smiles,
gathered their soggy hats and went home.

On the day of the Cross-country Races
the old mirror again fell asleep.
So the three hares piled on all their feathered hats.
They drove off proudly in their carriage
to watch the races through long-handled glasses.

"How lovely we look," they said.
"What beautiful hats,"
said a voice from behind their carriage.
"The plumes are so long and…and…
AAAAAAA-CHOOOOOOOO!"

TIPPLE! TIPPLE! TOPPLE! FLIP!
Down fell all the hats.
The hares smiled foolish smiles,
gathered their dusty hats and went home.

On the day of the Winter Carnival
the old mirror again fell asleep.
So the three hares heaped on all their fur hats
and drove off proudly in their sleigh.

"How elegant we look," they said to themselves
as they slid past snowmen.
Laughter, music, and snowballs
filled the icy air.
Suddenly, *BAM! PLOP! THUMP!*,
a shower of snowballs hit them and
TIPPLE! TIPPLE! TOPPLE! FLIP!
Down fell all the hats.
The three hares leaped from their sleigh
and dashed about madly,
throwing snowballs high,
and snowballs low,
and snowballs all about them.
"Great fun!" cried the three hares.
Then they bounded off again,
whooping, and laughing, and tumbling,
filling the air with more snowballs.

When everyone was tired, and puffing, and cold,
the three hares invited all of them home
for blackberry tarts and crumb cakes.

"What great fun!" cried the old mirror,
giggling, and blinking, and smiling.

And after that, the three hares
never had much time for their beautiful hats.
Oh, they wore them, of course, on wet or windy days.
But whenever they turned to their mirror, they would say,
"Mirror, Mirror, on the wall,
who are the three happiest hares of all?"
And the mirror was never too tired to smile back at them.

"Fiddle-dum! Fiddle-dee!" sang the Second Rabbit,
and he began his tale.

THE MERRY MINSTREL

Once there was a family of hares
who lived beside a cabbage patch.
All they ever did
was sit about eating cabbage soup.

17

But one little hare named Sniffer
did not like eating cabbage soup
again and again and again.
"Such a dull, stupid life," he wailed.
"Someday, I'm going to do something besides
sitting about eating cabbage soup.
I don't know what, and I don't know when,
but someday I'm going to do something
to make people laugh, and sing, and be happy."
"How dumb!" cried the other hares.
"Sit down and eat your soup."

So Sniffer sat down and ate his soup.

One day after he had grown a bit, *BANG!*
Sniffer threw down his spoon and shouted,
"I'm going to be a squirrel and eat acorns."
"Sit down and eat your soup," said his mother.

But Sniffer climbed an old oak tree in the forest
and he sat there eating acorns and yodeling to himself.
He sat and he ate and he yodeled
until one stormy night... *CRASH!*

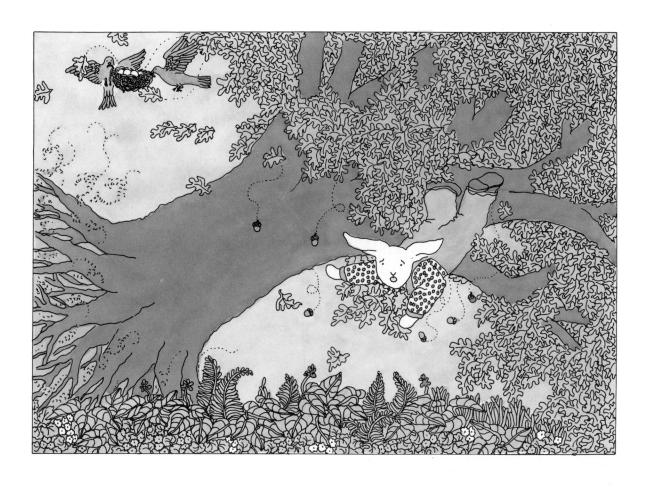

The tree fell over.
Sniffer hobbled home.
"Sit down and eat your soup," cried all the hares.

After three more days of cabbage soup,
Sniffer shouted, "I'm going to join the circus."
"You're mad!" cried all the hares.
"Sit down and eat your soup."

But Sniffer went off and joined the circus.
He did tumbles in the ring
and he danced with the dancing bears

until one stormy night...*CRASH!*
The big-top tent fell in.
Sniffer hobbled home.
"We told you so," cried all the hares.
"Eat your cabbage soup."

Then, one especially dull day at tea
(it was cabbage soup, of course),
Sniffer suddenly dashed off and up an oak tree
and began yodeling again.

Now he was prancing about
playing a tune on his fiddle.
"Fiddle-dum! Fiddle-dee!" he sang from the tree.

Next he was doing wild tumbles
and crazy flips.

Then he was dancing the Mexican Hat Dance.
"TA-DA! TA-DA! TA-DA!"

All the hares cheered and clapped
and sang and danced
until late in the night.

Early the next day, Sniffer waved good-bye
and went off to be a minstrel.
He wanted to make people laugh,
and sing, and be happy.
And Sniffer has been a minstrel ever since,
roving about, fiddling, and dancing,
and tumbling, and yodeling.

But on special occasions,
and sometimes for no good reason at all,
Sniffer comes home on the train
to visit and have a little cabbage soup.

The Third Rabbit blinked his eyes
and spoke very slowly.

THE MAGIC PILLOW

Once there was a small bunny
who lived in the country
and had nobody to play with.

Every day she helped in the kitchen,
played with her toys, and raked in the garden.
Then she ate her supper, went to bed,
put her head on her magic pillow,
and wished for a special dream.

One night she dreamed
she was a yellow balloon,
bobbing and floating in the air,
looking down on gardens,
and steeples,
and friendly people everywhere.

Another night she dreamed
she was the North Wind
with a smoky mustache,
calling little children out to play
in the flying leaves.

Other nights,
she dreamed she was
a scarecrow on Halloween...
the Queen of Hearts
snip-snip-snipping red valentines...
and a ballerina
whirling and twirling in pink shoes.

But her best dream
was a dream about a friend.

She and her friend would play in the park,
share a bag of candy, or just sit on a high hill
and watch the stars come out one by one.

One day she was raking,
and the small bunny met another small bunny
rolling down a grassy hill behind the garden.
They became the best of friends.
They played together every day
and told each other
all their dreams and secrets.
"My best dream has come true,"
said the small bunny.

After that
the small bunny never again wished a dream for herself.
But on a very special occasion
she would put her head on her magic pillow,
wish for a special dream,
wrap it,
and tie it,
and send it off to her new friend.

The Fourth Rabbit told his story
in a very tiny voice.

THE SHADOW AND THE WIND

One cold, windy day
two rabbits sat before the fire
with their father.
"Look," said Father,
"we can make shadow pictures on the wall."
And, with their paws,
they made lots and lots
of shadow pictures on the wall.

They made a butterfly...
a rabbit...
a giraffe.
Then Father said,
"I must go into the woodshed
for more firewood.
You stay here by the fire
and make more shadows on the wall."
And they did.

One small rabbit made a shadow on the wall.
The shadow became a hen
and danced about the room in the firelight.

Then the other rabbit made a shadow on the wall.
The shadow became a fox.
The fox saw the hen and began to chase it.

Around the room ran the hen.
Around the room ran the fox.
Out the door ran the hen.
Out the door ran the fox.

The two small rabbits laughed and giggled.
Then they heard something rattle the window
and say, "Whooooo."
"What was that?" asked one small rabbit
in a very tiny voice.
"It was the fox," said the other small rabbit
in a very shaky voice.
And both small rabbits were so frightened
they wouldn't let their father into the house.

The Fifth Rabbit smiled
and began.

FOOLISH RABBIT

Once there was a rabbit
who was so kind
that some people thought he was foolish.
One day
Foolish Rabbit went off to see the world
with a basket full of clothes
and good things to eat.
"Good-bye, my son," called Mother.
"Come home soon."

After a while it began to rain.
So Foolish Rabbit opened his umbrella
and splashed along
until he met someone with no umbrella.
"Hello, my friend," said Foolish Rabbit.
"Here, take my umbrella.
I love to feel the rain on my face."

The rain stopped and the hot sun came out.
Foolish Rabbit put on his straw hat
and marched along
until he met someone with no straw hat.
"Hello, my friend," said Foolish Rabbit.
"Here, take my straw hat.
I love to feel the sun on my head."

Foolish Rabbit traveled north and south,
east and west, giving everything away.
And one day, when his basket was empty,
Foolish Rabbit came to a fair.

Foolish Rabbit watched a clown.
And he rode on the merry-go-round.
And then he watched a juggler.
The juggler was very good.
He juggled five cups,
and twirled four hoops,
and whirled three balls,
all at the same time.
THEN...
the juggler juggled seven invisible balls.
Or so he said.
Foolish Rabbit clapped politely.

The juggler tried to trick Foolish Rabbit.
"Do you know how much
    these seven invisible balls are worth?"
he asked.
"Hmmm!" said Foolish Rabbit,
    wrinkling his forehead.
"They must be worth their weight in gold."
"Sold!" shouted the juggler. "Pay me."

"Yes, indeed,"
said Foolish Rabbit with a smile.
"Here is a basket full of invisible gold."
And he handed the empty basket to the juggler.

Then Foolish Rabbit went home whistling
to tell his mother all about the world.

THE SIXTH TALE

"Now for the sixth tale,"
  said the conductor,
  who had sat down
  to hear all the stories.
  But the only sound was a snore.
  The Sixth Rabbit was fast asleep.
"Oh dear!" cried the other rabbits.
"Now we will never know
  whose tale is best.
  And we will never know
  who won the basket of Easter eggs."

And they never did.
For soon
  there were six rabbits snoring happily.

"Good night, my friends,"
whispered the conductor
as he dimmed the lights.
"And, since I did all the listening,
thank you for the basket full
of delicious Easter eggs."